LIFE AFTER ADVANCED LEVEL DIARIES

First Diary

THE DAWN OF A NEW ERA

Shadreck Masawi

TalNet Independent Publishers
Harare Zimbabwe

ISBN: 9781779068996

First published: June 2019
Published by: TalNet Independent Publishers
Printed by: TalNet Printers

Life after Advanced Level Series

Volume 1: The Dawn of a new era
Volume 2: First Mission, Searching for Love
Volume 3: when you find love
Volume 4:
Volume 5:

INTRODUCTION

What really came into your mind the first time you received an acceptance letter from a University or College of your choice? Did your heart communicate something to you? Did your toes freeze? Did you feel excited? We know that something really happened that day. It's good for you who had already witnessed the Life after Advanced level. This is the first part of the novel; *Life after Advanced Level Series*. It digs deeper into an environment one can experience or expect to experience during the first days as a student on his/her way to become a graduate. But remember everyone has his or her own story to tell at the end, which is designed by the environment one chooses to shape his/her life after Advanced level at.

DISCLAIMER

The names of the characters in this Novel were inspired by the students whom I met at Great Zimbabwe University but the events did not by any chance relate to the behaviour or life of these people who had their names appearing in this novel. The location of the story bears the names from Masvingo Province but most of the geographical features are not from the Province.

DEDICATION

This First part of the Novel is dedicated to Stanley Kwangwa, Crispen Nyadenga, Gerald Sibindi, Ruvimbo Makoni, Patience Muteranduwa, Esinath Chagonda, Christine Kunaka, and Thembinkosi Woyo. These were the first guys I first got in touch with when I started my Bachelor's Degree in Development Studies at Great Zimbabwe University.

EPISODE ONE

Welcome to the University of Choice

The morning was becoming warm in March, and earlier that evening, cold breeze had swirled about the squares of the campus and parks around. In the comfort of the sofas in the apartments lounge, however, all was jollity for the two girls who had re-united after a long period of separation. Their union was boisterous and enthusiastic, and even became more welcomed as they bared their *experiences*. Many *diverted* glances came their way, glances not touched by admiration, but of detection for they presented an attractive *courtesy*.

Delighted by this unexpected meeting, and full of youthful high spirits, they shortly forgot their surroundings. Their voices rose up making some of the college girls to continuously frown in their direction. Ruvimbo one of the two had her blur eyes alighted with this, suggested in a stage whisper that they should *adjourn* to her room.

"Your room!" Christine replied in a high tone still full of double aged happiness.

"Yeh my room, we are almost drawing attention of everyone here." *She then flicks her hands sideways.*

"Ok beautiful, you know that I always take your word with respect, let's go upstairs to your room." *She gave a smile looking at her friend.*

They picked themselves from the consolation of the sofas which were lined in the lounge and went upstairs to Ruvimbo's room. Though the subject was all about their bygones, the stories snaked also to the perfect moment they were going to have at the new place.

Going up stairs did not stop the two from exhuming their past. They were still young ladies who had separated for a long time. They now met behind the University premises and it became the greatest opportunity for them to dig deeper into their past.

Ruvimbo at this time of her life was a *meagre* vessel, full of emotions shrouded by series of smiles which exposes her little dimples out, which makes it difficult for many people to detect whether she was in good mood or not. She had an instant justice policy were she did not wait for another day to come and solve issues troubling her. Her Manyika dialect was in her tongue to some extent, despite the fact that she had spent her advanced level at St John's Chikwaka, one of the boarding schools in Goromonzi District Mashonaland East Province: the characteristics cadence of that dialect from her Manicaland Province being voiced by the syllable W, the tone which most people laugh at. Most people who came from that Province were known as the Wasu people.

She was a good-looking girl of the age of 20, with a difficult to actually guess her age, because of her face which has rebuked growth. She had a sexy body with curved hips, and small rounded breast pointing to the front, a round face blessed with sexy lips. A lady clouded in light in complexion. In reality, she was beautiful as in natural, nothing deserved to be subtracted from her.

Phrases of her childhood lurked in her aspect still. As she walked along today, with her bouncing real womanhood, you could sometimes see her fifteenth birthday in her cheeks, or her tenth year sparkling in her eyes, even her sixteenth seen in her smiles, now and then. That's why she was called a tower of beauty where everyone could easily see from a distance.

Her friendship with Christine was a combination of two beautiful girls destined to seduce the opposite sex. Christine was a lady in her early 20s. She was medium in complexion, well-structured with an admirable sexy body which was destined to cause commotion inside manhood. Unlike her friend, she was slim and relatively tall with outstanding breast. She had a structure of a true African woman who valued her culture most. If it was in the ancient times, she would have qualified to be married to royalty and not suitable for *kuripangozi*.

Hence, it was a strong combination between a true African lady destined to her culture and one from the western world.

Outside the hostel rooms, the wind was blowing savagely from all angles, with early morning warmth giving a momentum disappearance to the dew which was settling on the flowers and lawn. Delimited by a Dura hall were the houses of the students, with the next Dura hall harbouring some of the University premises. In cream body and red roofs, the nicest slice of paradise was tossed down to take part as hostels. Those who ministered at the residence were already hard at work cleaning the rooms and the entire complex, extending their honour to the beauty of the campus.

Twittering and less irritating sounds fabricated by the birds were welcoming a new day, with a family of Bees entertaining themselves with sweet juice from the flowers around.

The morning mist gradually vanished; with wonderful beauties of the University clearly seen from a distance standing on the high ground.

Great Zimbabwe University lay amid in the western undulations of the beautiful city of Masvingo. A well-built land sets its attractive and gorgeous look at the zenith of a high ground, providing a perfect look from a distance, a tower of beauty where everyone would love to witness. It was bounded North by Madzimbahwe Teachers College. To its South, the blooming and evergreen rainy season vegetation embraces the prominence of Chiremba Hill, blessed with beautiful mansions beneath? Moving westwards after a score of some miles over calcareous ups and downs, the rain season flooded Nyagui River present itself, a jack of all trades. The University draws most of its water for irrigation from this river. Most lovebirds also favoured this place as a hideout, where the waterfalls and fresh air from the river entertained them. Just after the river, about a couple of miles away, there was a presentation of an open landscape where the midday sun blazes, giving an unclipped character to the land and the atmosphere.

The clock ticked and hit 8:30, in the morning with the sun shining lightly emanating from the shades of the clouds, giving a warm Tuesday early, though few strata were still showing themselves above. There was a clear indication that the bright light piercing through the clouds was going to extend its temperature for the rest of the day, an assurance by *climatologist*.

About a quarter of the Bachelors and Spinsters were still dreaming, with the rest already pleasing themselves with assorted activities of the day. Some were busy looking at the places around, with others still accommodated in their rooms preparing to help their complaining intestines. No one among the wise brides of the new day was left motionless.

The cry of the siren turned out the whole joy and excitements to another set of moment. *Like a child dragged home at the peak of the entertainment*, thus how the atmosphere was after the cry of the siren. It carried the minds of the new students to the high school days were bells and sirens were sounded signifying many things, break, and lunch among others. For now, they failed to come up with a good answer of what it meant. As per tradition the siren was blown here, ply on emergence meetings were the attention of students was urgently needed. For now, the Great Hall was awaiting for them.

For a decade, the Great Hall was situated on a stony place, some meters east of the Hostels in the next Dura hall. It was an enormous Hall exemplifying the Great States Buildings, the kind that brought many to an excitement, on their first sight which deserved such comments as, "*this building has brought me to the western world*." depending on oneself. Despite its vast size, it had a simple charm, the hiring of the best architectures around the country to give an excellent building like this one. The graceful gables and beautiful windows, the well-designed walls prevailed from a distance adding to its beautifulness.

Like most buildings at various institutions around, the rooms *skipped* inside leaving a much bigger space at the other end where important gatherings were conducted. It was built in a story like manner where the room which was usually used for mass meetings was at the ground flow. Going upstairs, there were some rooms to conduct special Lectures and some few offices up there. Thus, it deserves the name, the Great Hall.

In a space of time, all the students *mustered* around in the comfort of the chairs which were arranged in an ascending order from the front.

This was made easier for those who sat at the back to clearly hear and see the one who will be addressing at the podium.

Chin resting on one hand, elbow resting on the arms of the chair, Ruvimbo and her friend were part of those who had attended the meeting with nothing bothering them, except waiting for an unpredicted moment to come. This was going to be their first in time at the University to be addressed in mass.

"This room is nice." Ruvimbo commented looking at her friend and then around the room again.

"Everything here is awesome; I wonder why most students were running away from this Institute." Now her eyes were running around, adjusting at all angles of the room.

"Let's wait and see how knowledge package is here."

Their voices competing with the environment makes the two girls to quickly retire from their conversation and left the floor to their eyes. Everything they were capturing was looking new, great, giving them a fantasy thought that they were at the right place indeed.

The whole room was fully blasted with noise made by the students which makes communication more difficult for them as each person tried to talk high for his or her partner to remain in the conversation. The noise waved from one side to the other, which was a clear indication that they were talking about the new environment, whilst expressing their excitements.

The presentation of a young, energetic and handsome man at the *dais* alighted the whole room to turn into the house of admiration. He was wearing a black suit matching green stripped tie and blue shirt, not knowing what he was putting on foot as the podium hide his half bottom body. He was light in complexion, with his hair well done, his body matching himself, without any traces of jealousy he was really a handsome man.

"Silence please." He makes his first impression this way. "May you all please pay attention; we don't want to waste much of your precious time." He voiced from the microphone exposing his white tooth outside, and arranged a bunch of papers he was holding as if he was a newsreader. The students stopped talking at once giving him the time. He then carried on with his address. "I welcome you all to the most beautiful University, the University of Excellence, the greatest weapon in education as the name implies." He paused for a moment looking at the students who were who appreciated his words. "I am here on behalf of the University staff members to welcome you all in the name of our faithful God. It is written, in everything you do in life, God should lead you. Before we start our program of the day, I would like call upon Mrs Munyavi to the stage to give us an opening prayer". He then paused with his eyes locating for Mrs Munyavi.

Students began to clap hands welcoming a short and bulge woman to the stage to give a word of prayer. All the students kept quiet as the woman prayed.

After a short prayer, the master of ceremony returned to the podium to continue with his speech which was mixed with funny chants and monkey actions. He then calls upon the Vice Chancellor Professor Zvogbo to give a speech before attending welcome meetings at other campuses. A round of applause follows as students welcomes him.

Called out to come to the floor, ululations and whistles covered the Hall in outburst of joy, with students welcoming the Deputy Head of the University

The Vice Chancellor gave out the long awaited speech to the students. Though his speech was short, it was a mixture of facts and jokes making the speech more interesting and motivating again. In short, it was there to market the University using the tongue.

After the Vice Chancellors speech, there come other staff members from different disciplines to deliver their speeches giving a balance to both academic and non-academic cycles.

After a series of speeches, all the attending students were shown around the college premises especially those related to academics before they were released to prepare for the following morning tour. Ruvimbo and Christine were among other students, they did not want anything to leave them shadowed.

EPISODE TWO

The Student Tourist

The morning after day one of *compass reading*, students *convene* all over from the hostels, to every corner in and outside the campus. Most of them were talking about the day they were going to spend viewing the exciting places around. It was a good time their eyes were going to tell their hearts the story behind the University tradition.

The sun was mounting from the east, giving a sudden disappearance of the dew, with a glimpse of light shining beyond the eastern horizon. Birds of the air were already singing the songs of sensation in welcoming the new day. The morning temperature was hot promising a hot day light. It was some hours after a *bunch* of witches had retired from their evening hunt.

Students were in their special outfits, which gave them a clear glance of maturity, as they wait for the buses to come and ferry them. It looked as if every student was in his/her specialty, well prepared to tour around for the rest of the day.

It was a sacrosanct moment for all the first year students to spend their second day at the University visiting the interesting places around. A day like this one was a ritual event, done specifically for the first year students as a special way of welcoming them to a new life at the University. At the same time, some critics could actually say, a special time to win the hearts of many students.

This was going to be a memorable moment, not to be forgotten in their life at the University. To those who had never visited the country's wonders, it was going to be the most exciting day out, fulfilling what they have learnt from childhood about the wonders of the country, especially Great Zimbabwe Ruins where the country's name was derived from. Though part of entertainment, to some it was going to be a *spring,* especially those who were undergoing programs related to culture and heritage. Thus, the day calls for a total celebration and the event perfect to be written in their lifetime diaries.

At 8o'clock arithmetic proven, the buses were already at the campus picking points, ready to ferry the students. There were five buses, which all were designated for this programme of the day. It did not claim half an hour time for the buses to be fully loaded. After close to an hour of travelling with students full of good spirits, they all arrived safely at their first touring destination, the Great Zimbabwe ruins.

All proceedings were carefully conducted for the students to be allowed to enter and tour the wonderful site of the Great Madzimbahwe. Excitement gestures and endless debates crowded the whole area with students asking each other about the anonymous structures their eyes were going to enjoy for the first time. Some went on to ask about the mysterious things they read in the books.

At the entrance gate, a welcoming large signpost was laminated showing the map of the ruins directions and positions of certain structures which were inside, with *humus* of tour guides stationed there waiting to take the *tourist* on a tour. Everything from the outside looked great, master-casing what was inside.

After few minutes of preparations, the *tourists* were allowed access under the *role* of different tour guides, being divided into groups. They walked in a processional way, introducing themselves inside, and will then spread, each one in comfort zone in the deep corners of the good *yard*. They walked for few miles away from the entrance and reached their first station, a small and well-built refreshment bar where the tour guide gave a free play to those who wanted to satisfy their intestines giving a taste to the mouth. This also marked the first mission of the tour guide, as he enlightens them about the whole ruins in phases.

The first exhibition was in a processional orderly like march up hill with the students following the tour guide. It was not difficult to distinguish between the Adams and the Eves generations, as the Eve formed indeed the majority of those who were walking behind, with the Adams leading upfront. Their heads of luxuriating hair were reflected in the sunshine, with most of them wearing shining earrings on their ears. A difficult of arranging their lips in the crude exposes them to the public scrutiny and inability to balance their heads and dissociate self-consciousness from their features, was apparent to them, showing that they were real college girls accustomed to many eyes.

Although the distance from the hilltop was short, many students lost energy because of its heart-breaking steepness. Most of the *tourists*, especially from the *dresses* apartment were already tired with some even not willing to make another step forward.

From the top, the aerial view of the land beneath was clearly casted out, exposing the whole of it into the natural eyes of the tourist. Looking southwards, a Great Enclosure separated from the hill by a valley was clearly seen. To the east, the ancient village was showing itself on the dwala, an area which resembled the ancient time villages of the Shona communities. The western side close to the entrance was blessed with a museum.

Hilltop, the students were enjoying the beauty of the area. Various play grounds where found there, including the curve, which was debated to be used as storage of the tools, the king's *Dare* and many others. This is the same place where the famous rejuvenating therapy tree well known as *Muchemedza-mbuya* was found. The Camera's sounds were heard ticking randomly from all directions with flashlights igniting the completely stone structures, with some funny clips being taken which were going to be used as evidence that they were at Great Zimbabwe Ruins to the doubting Thomas's.

It was also a mixture of grief, pain and a little bit of happiness among others. Some were already complaining about their itching legs, with others complaining about the blazing fire ignited from the sun with others crying for food.

One, from the Eves dynasty found herself seating down outside, feeling every pain in her body as others proceeded down-hill.

'Wow! I'm tired,' she sighed relaxing under a small tree, which provided her with little shed from the burning sun. No one seemed to entertain her but rather surprised to see her as they pass by.

Suddenly, Christine came to a sudden halt and looked at her. "What are you doing here?" she asked Ruvimbo who was busy playing with her own thoughts.

Ruvimbo raised her head and smiled. "Oh you are back! I'm okay; it's only that I am trying to ease my itching legs and also waiting for you to come."

She stared at her for some seconds before saying another word. She then gripped this - "this girl is too weak; she cannot afford to take another step by herself. I used to walk 15km to and from school every day. That's why it is said life is different for sure." she glanced at her again feeling sorry, "Ok, I think you rested enough lets go now."

No problem, we can go now I think I had rested enough also." she replied trying to pick herself up.

"Give me your hand." she stretched her hand and helped her up.

"Thanks." she replied holding her hand to comfortably and picked herself up.

"The pleasure is mine"

She took her purse from the ground and they started to walk downhill using a different path from the former. The paths to the Hill Complex were many so one simply chooses which one he/she liked to follow. They walked some few meters without exchanging voices. They were the only ones who were left behind whilst others were already in the path which led them through the valley surrounded by brown grass and shrubs, heading towards the ancient village.

As they were walking, Ruvimbo came to a sudden stop. "Now you can go and join others, I will wait for you here." She said looking at Christine whilst holding her waist.

"What?" She paused for a moment looking back at her. "I cannot leave you here alone. I'm no longer interested to go another mile again, let's wait until they come back."

"Why are you denying yourself the joy you have been offered? It's only that I'm tired otherwise I wouldn't be here."

"No I can't leave you alone." Insisted Christine.

"OK if you insist. I was not chasing you away, I was just doing it for you, so let's go and have a seat over there."

"The whole walking thing is not my thing bae. I only walked back home because I wanted to learn and I am here because this trip is something we as first year students should be doing together and missing it would definitely *drink*.'

As they were talking, they came close to the kiosk and they suggested having some refreshments before proceeding to have a perfect sit on the benches which were under the trees.

The sky was *surrendered* in blue, with a warm if not hot smooth flowing heat carried sideways. There was no much difference between those who were exposed in the sun and those under the trees, only the rate of heat differed regularly.

Being differentiated from other areas, the province of Masvingo was well known for being one of the hottest areas in the country. It was a mother to a small rural area of Zaka well known as *Zakarinopisa,* literally meaning the hot area. Not so many people liked the area because of its high temperatures. That is why the area was well known for its vast lands suitable only for at least cattle rearing. When it comes to winter season, its temperatures varied regularly from too cold to high temperatures.

"These people are too strong, they are still fighting in the sun like this, to make matters worse, others reached the extension of not removing their nylons." Ruvimbo broke the silence taking the last sip of coke down her neck.

"With all this excitements of touring around our *country*, they can't feel it." Christine replied repositioning herself on the bench.

"Um! But it's too hard to undertake, maybe you can say so."

"Woooow ! At last they are coming. Seating here was now tiresome"

"I think they had a great time. Look at those sun baked faces." said Christine looking at other students who were now coming from the direction of the museum.

After having a good time at the Hill complex, the students proceeded to the ancient village where they were welcomed by the traditional shona community and traditional dance. From the village, they went straight to the great enclosure before they come to the museum.

"I think my being tired relished you to escape the cruel heat, otherwise I would have not recognised you." She replied with a mocking smile.

With that said, Christine did not say anything, she just smiled back.

"I hope I didn't offend you my dear, you will get used to me that's who I am." said Ruvimbo staring at Christine. "Hope you haven't forgotten"

"Not really, I am not that type who can be easily offended by silly things. I think you know me better."

As they were still talking, students were filing past them and something captured Ruvimbo's attention, "Christine, look at that boy walking ahead of us." She said hurriedly pointing to a lonely boy walking in front of them.

"I can locate him well, what's wrong with him?"

"What did you notice?"

"His step of course" Christine said with a little giggling smile mounted on her face.

"Yep, imagine being proposed by such a guy, what would you honestly do?" She asked trying to employ seriousness on her face.

With a mocking laughter, "what's wrong with this guy? I will just accept if my heart is magnetised to his. Disability does not mean inability my dear; He is just a human being like you and a man too."

"Wow! You are one in a million; I don't even want to see his tooth out for me. If he proposed, I would die." Ruvimbo mocked throwing her hands windically.

"Don't say that my friend, you don't know how your children will be presented to you in the real world."

Ruvimbo went on teasing and making funny of the boy.

"Look my dear, I'm not going to walk another inch of step with you if you mock that boy again." She finally warned her friend.

With that, Ruvimbo broke into laughter, which drew the attention of most of the students. In a moment, her eyes became little moist, and her glance dropped to the ground so she could not meet the eyes of those whom she had attentioned. Embroidered in a good manner, she proudly recovered to equanimity and she then tapped her old friend on the shoulder and proceeded to occupy a perfect place fit for two waiting for another tour.

Among the onlookers, were three boys of the same age with varying heights. On their shoulders, they were carrying Laptop bags, with their left hands, carrying empty water bottles, listening to each step they took outside the gate with confidence of being real college boys. They seemed to be brothers from different mothers, if not, they were friends with tact. They had nothing to worry about, except complaining about the blazing sunny day.

They stood by the gate side, waiting to boarder the bus to another exciting place to come. They inquired to the beauty of the girls who were passing by, seeming to be on a screening process of the beautiful ladies. No one bothers to talk to one another, surgically clear that they were all tired from the day's long tour.

One of the boys who seemed to be young and short from others, was leaning by the pillar next to the entrance gate, folding his hands with his right leg over left. He would have been hardly characterized. There was an uncurbed, unchained aspect in his eyes and attire implying that he had wholly found the entrance of his professional groove, that he was a desultory tentative student of something and that all the proceedings might only have been predicted for him. From a distance, one could easily identify that he was a man full of himself determined to a greater future.

The other two who were tall with relative characteristics, *chuz'* pliant not to intend to linger more than a movement or pay attention to the beautiful of the girls who were *vexing* around. They were leaning on the security fence with their hands in the pockets, with empty bottles dumped between their legs.

The spectacle of the bevy of girls who walked behind others, without male partners seemed to amuse the third guy.

He looked at each step they took passing, with only smiles seen from a distance assuming that they were having a great moment. He turned his eyes to his friends and whispered, "Look guys, the beautiful angels passing by." now pointing to the girls.

"You have started again Stunner, until when will you stop showing us the nude girls of yours, whatever you call them?" the other boy responded recklessly.

"That's all you can say Crispen, can't you see that they are distinctive girls destined for white weddings, am I lying Anesu?" he said turning to the other guy who was still in a moment of silent trying to figure out the girls correctly.

"I think for now you are totally correct, these girls are hot. If I figured out correctly they deserve to be called blackberry girls for sure." Anesu echoed relaxing himself leaning on the fence.

"What else can you say Anesu except to echo what Stunner has said?" exclaimed Crispen fetching his empty water bottle from between his legs.

"Come on Cris, everything good deserves a comment."

"So what are you going to do now guys, these are truly beautiful girls, they deserve sweetest guys like us, they broke my heart Woooo." said Stunner holding his chest, in a deep sensation of a dreaming lover boy.

"I'm inclined to go and have a chat with them. Why not all of us just go for some few minutes, it will not detain us long.?" responded Anesu in a pace to go.

"Now you are reasoning like grown-ups guys, that's a brilliant idea lets go." Stunner expressed his enthusiasm to have a chat with the girls.

"Hold on to that! I think you are going alone as you can see, you two are matching the girls." expressed Crispen feeling relaxed.

The two boys turned back to Crispen who was still glued to the pillar behind, with no passion to go. Anesu looked at him. "Why?" He asked surprisingly.

"As you can see guys I am tired I can't afford to have another step chasing after the Eve's dynasty, so you can go, I will be waiting." He then stared at his friends who were now paralyzed by his reply.

"So we can leave you behind, here is my bag, we will come and take you here." said Anesu handing his laptop bag to Crispen.

"But why are we leaving him here? Can't you see that I'm not worthwhile to engage into any relation with one of the girls I was just doing it for you two." Stunner excused himself professionally.

"Hold on, so you were just doing it for us not you?" Crispen said with a mocking smile on his face. "And as a matter of fact I never said I am not interested, the thing is, I am tired, and these girls with their beauties, they need a man with all his energy or else they will embarrass us here, so let's do the hunt tomorrow whilst not in a hurry like this."

"Ey! You guys surprised me woo. I didn't know that you behave this way when you see girls." Anesu convened heartbroken slapping his friend on the face verbally.

"It's ok Anesu, we will do it tomorrow, see that the buses are ready now, let's go. I don't want to have a bad seat." cheered Stunner *tapping* Anesu on the shoulder who was standing insentient beside him being seduced, unromantically by his friend's decision.

Notes

Notes

Notes

Notes